The
Three Little Pigs
and the
New Neighbor

Written by Andy Blackford

Illustrated by Tomislav Zlatic

Crabtree Publishing Company

www.crabtreebooks.com

Crabtree Publishing Company
www.crabtreebooks.com
1-800-387-7650

PMB 59051, 350 Fifth Ave.   616 Welland Ave.
59th Floor,   St. Catharines, ON
New York, NY 10118   L2M 5V6

Published by Crabtree Publishing in 2014

Series editor: Melanie Palmer
Editor: Crystal Sikkens
Notes to adults: Reagan Miller
Series advisor: Catherine Glavina
Series designer: Peter Scoulding
Production coordinator and
   Prepress technician: Margaret Amy Salter
Print coordinator: Margaret Amy Salter

Text © Andy Blackford 2010
Illustrations © Tomislav Zlatic 2010

First published in 2010
by Franklin Watts
(A division of Hachette
Children's Books)

Printed in the
U.S.A./092014/CG20140808

**Library and Archives Canada
Cataloguing in Publication**

Blackford, Andy, author
       The three little pigs and the new neighbor /
written by Andy Blackford ; illustrated by Tomislav
Zlatic.

(Tadpoles: fairytale twists)
Issued in print and electronic formats.
ISBN 978-0-7787-0447-8 (bound).--ISBN 978-0-7787-
0482-9 (pbk.).--ISBN 978-1-4271-7567-0 (pdf).--ISBN
978-1-4271-7559-5 (html)

       I. Zlatic, Tomislav, illustrator II. Title.

PZ7.B532Th 2014   j823'.92   C2013-908335-9
                                                        C2013-908336-7

**Library of Congress
Cataloging-in-Publication Data**

CIP available at Library of Congress

This story is based on the traditional fairy tale,
The Three Little Pigs, but with a new twist.
Can you make up your own twist for the story?

Once there were three little pigs.
One lived in a house made of straw,
one lived in a house made of sticks,
and one in a house made of bricks.

STRAW VILLA

Brick House

STICK TOWER

3

One day, a new neighbor moved
in next door to the straw house.
"Oh no!" cried the little pig.
"It's the Big Bad Wolf!"

All day the wolf worked hard,
sorting out his new home.
"Now I'm hungry," he said, and
prepared himself a tasty dinner.

But he knocked over the pepper
shaker. The pepper went
everywhere!

The wolf coughed and sneezed and choked on all the pepper. It even got in his eyes.

"I need water," he gasped, "but I haven't got any! Perhaps that little pig next door will help me."

9

The wolf knocked on the
first little pig's door.

The pig was so scared,
he squealed, "Go away!
There's nobody home!"

The wolf knocked harder. But the door was only made of straw, so his paw went right through.

The little pig ran to his brother's house made of sticks.

"Help! Let me in! The Big Bad Wolf is after me!" he squealed.

"Oh no!" wheezed the wolf.
"There's no one at home.
I'll try next door. The little
pig there might help me."

15

The wolf knocked on the door, and the two little pigs quickly hid.

"Let me in!" the wolf sputtered. But no one answered. "Maybe there's someone upstairs," he thought and went to climb up.

STICK
TOWER

19

But the wolf was heavy, and the house was only made of sticks. The roof broke, and he fell right through!

"Oh dear! What a mess!"
the wolf groaned.
"Perhaps the little pig
next door will help me."

The two little pigs ran next door
to their brother's house.
"Help!" they cried. "The Big
Bad Wolf is trying to eat us up!"

As the wolf knocked on the door,
the third little pig shouted:
"Go away! My house is made
of bricks! You'll never get in
and eat us up!"

"But I don't want to eat you up!
I only want some water!" coughed
the wolf.

27

The three little pigs laughed. Then they gave the wolf as much water as he could drink, and plenty more!

Puzzle 1

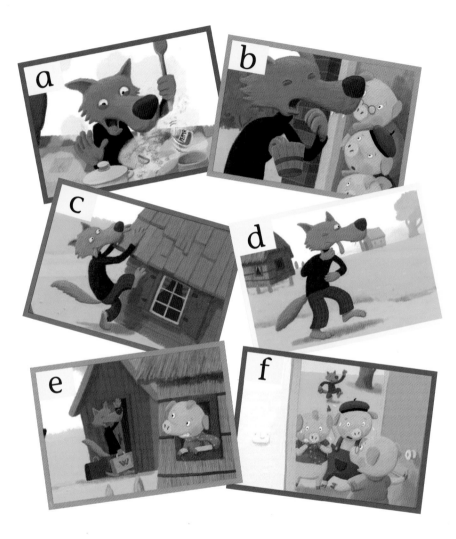

Put these pictures in the correct order. Which
event is the most important? Try writing the
story in your own words. Use your imagination
to put your own "twist" on the story!

Puzzle 2

1. I'm very hungry.

2. Here is what the wolf needs.

3. I need to escape!

4. I must find some water.

5. I'm scared of being eaten!

6. It's hard work moving to a new house.

Match the speech bubbles to the correct character in the story. Turn the page to check your answers.

Notes for adults

TADPOLES: Fairytale Twists are engaging, imaginative stories designed for early fluent readers. The books may also be used for read-alouds or shared reading with young children.

TADPOLES: Fairytale Twists are humorous stories with a unique twist on traditional fairy tales. Each story can be compared to the original fairy tale, or appreciated on its own. Fairy tales are a key type of literary text found in the Common Core State Standards.

THE FOLLOWING PROMPTS BEFORE, DURING, AND AFTER READING SUPPORT LITERACY SKILL DEVELOPMENT AND CAN ENRICH SHARED READING EXPERIENCES:

1. **Before Reading**: Do a picture walk through the book, previewing the illustrations. Ask the reader to predict what will happen in the story. For example, ask the reader what he or she thinks the twist in the story will be.
2. **During Reading**: Encourage the reader to use context clues and illustrations to determine the meaning of unknown words or phrases.
3. **During Reading**: Have the reader stop midway through the book to revisit his or her predictions. Does the reader wish to change his or her predictions based on what they have read so far?
4. **During and After Reading**: Encourage the reader to make different connections:
   Text-to-Text: How is this story similar to/different from other stories you have read?
   Text-to-World: How are events in this story similar to/different from things that happen in the real world?
   Text-to-Self: Does a character or event in this story remind you of anything in your own life?
5. **After Reading**: Encourage the child to reread the story and to retell it using his or her own words. Invite the child to use the illustrations as a guide.

HERE ARE OTHER TITLES FROM TADPOLES: FAIRYTALE TWISTS FOR YOU TO ENJOY:

Cinderella's Big Foot	978-0-7787-0440-9 RLB	978-0-7787-0448-5 PB
Jack and the Bean Pie	978-0-7787-0441-6 RLB	978-0-7787-0449-2 PB
Little Bad Riding Hood	978-0-7787-0442-3 RLB	978-0-7787-0450-8 PB
Princess Frog	978-0-7787-0443-0 RLB	978-0-7787-0452-2 PB
Sleeping Beauty—100 Years Later	978-0-7787-0444-7 RLB	978-0-7787-0479-9 PB
The Lovely Duckling	978-0-7787-0445-4 RLB	978-0-7787-0480-5 PB
The Princess and the Frozen Peas	978-0-7787-0446-1 RLB	978-0-7787-0481-2 PB

VISIT WWW.CRABTREEBOOKS.COM FOR OTHER CRABTREE BOOKS.

Answers
Puzzle 1
The correct order is: 1e, 2a, 3d, 4c, 5f, 6b

Puzzle 2
The Big Bad Wolf: 1, 4, 6

The three little pigs: 2, 3, 5